Edgewise

Eliza Clark

A SAMUEL FRENCH ACTING EDITION

SAMUEL FRENCH

FOUNDED 1830

SAMUELFRENCH.COM
SAMUELFRENCH-LONDON.CO.UK

FOR PRODUCTION ENQUIRIES

UNITED STATES AND CANADA
Info@SamuelFrench.com
1-866-598-8449

UNITED KINGDOM AND EUROPE
Plays@SamuelFrench-London.co.uk
020-7255-4302

Each title is subject to availability from Samuel French, depending upon country of performance. Please be aware that *EDGEWISE* may not be licensed by Samuel French in your territory. Professional and amateur producers should contact the nearest Samuel French office or licensing partner to verify availability.

MUSIC USE NOTE

Licensees are solely responsible for obtaining formal written permission from copyright owners to use copyrighted music in the performance of this play and are strongly cautioned to do so. If no such permission is obtained by the licensee, then the licensee must use only original music that the licensee owns and controls. Licensees are solely responsible and liable for all music clearances and shall indemnify the copyright owners of the play(s) and their licensing agent, Samuel French, against any costs, expenses, losses and liabilities arising from the use of music by licensees. Please contact the appropriate music licensing authority in your territory for the rights to any incidental music.

IMPORTANT BILLING AND CREDIT REQUIREMENTS

If you have obtained performance rights to this title, please refer to your licensing agreement for important billing and credit requirements.

EDGEWISE had its world premeire at Walkerspace on November 9, 2010 in New York City. The production was produced by Page 73 Productions (Liz Jones and Asher Richelli, Executive Directors) and The Play Company (Kate Loewald, Founding Producer). The performance was directed by Trip Cullman, with sets by Andromache Chalfant, costumes by Jenny Mannis, sound by Bart Fasbender, and lighting by Nicole Pearce. The Production Stage Manager was Kelly Glasgow. The cast was as follows:

RUCKUS . . . . Philip Ettinger

MARCO . . . . Tobias Segal

EMMA . . . . Aja Naomi King

LOUIS . . . . .Alfredo Narciso

PAUL . . . . .Brandon Dirden

An earlier version of *EDGEWISE* was presented at the Cherry Lane Studio Theatre produced by Jeremy Robbins and Marisol Rosa-Shapiro and directed by Lila Neugebauer, July 25 - August 9, 2008.

CHARACTERS

RUCKUS – 17
MARCO – 17
EMMA – 17
LOUIS – 28
PAUL – early 20s

PLACE

Dougal's, a fast food joint.

TIME

Just east of the present.

Scene One

(The fluorescent lights come up one by one. A loud "on" sound accompanies each light. We are in a fast food joint — the audience's vantage point is from behind the counter, but we can see over the counter to the door, and the tables with their appetizing yellow tabletops. Far upstage, we may even be able to catch a glimpse of the linoleum floor. The place beyond the counter is glistening.)

(Behind the counter is a different story. A fryer on one wall, at the moment turned off, is covered in grease. The wastebasket next to it is brimming with cheeseburger wrappers, paper cups, lids, and cigarette butts. There is a drive-thru window with a cheap swiveling chair. A steel table in the corner must be where the employees package the food.)

(There is a door next to the fryer that leads into a storeroom.)

*(**COLIN RUCKER** has turned on the lights. He is a seventeen-year-old, messy-haired, foul-mouthed kid, and he goes by **RUCKUS**.)*

*(In turning on the lights, **RUCKUS** reveals **MARCO**, another seventeen-year-old boy who wears the Dougal's uniform, sitting on the floor behind the counter staring at the wall.)*

(It is early morning. Six o'clock maybe.)

RUCKUS. Dude. What are you doing?

(no response)

Marco. Yo Dickwad.

(beat)

RUCKUS. *(cont.)* Marco.

(**MARCO** *looks at him.*)

How long have you been here?

MARCO. I just got here.

RUCKUS. What are you doing on the floor?

MARCO. Sitting.

RUCKUS. Yeah. I see that.

MARCO. I'm tired, man. I'm just sitting.

RUCKUS. Did you turn the fryer on?

MARCO. It's heating.

RUCKUS. The fryer isn't on.

MARCO. It's heating.

RUCKUS. It's not heating, Marco. You didn't turn it on. Dude you gotta turn the fryer on or we can't open on time.

MARCO. I fucking turned the fryer on.

RUCKUS. Okay, Jesus. What's wrong with you?

MARCO. Nothing.

RUCKUS. You wanna smoke before we open?

MARCO. No.

RUCKUS. Why not?

MARCO. Emma smelled it last time. She doesn't want us to jeopardize her job.

RUCKUS. My dad doesn't come in on Saturdays.

MARCO. You're not the one who'd get fired.

RUCKUS. Dude, let me handle Emma. You look like you could use something.

MARCO. Someone got killed on the highway.

RUCKUS. Car crash?

MARCO. Shot, I think.

RUCKUS. You see some blood or something, Marco? You feel queasy?

MARCO. I'm fine, Dickhead. Leave me alone.

RUCKUS. You seen my hat?

MARCO. What hat?

RUCKUS. My manager hat.

MARCO. You made manager?

RUCKUS. Last night, baby.

MARCO. Fuckin' nepotism.

RUCKUS. Nepe-what?

MARCO. Nepotism. It's when someone makes his son manager even though he's retarded.

RUCKUS. You're the one all comatose and shit on the floor of a Dougal's. Get up and turn the fucking fryer on.

MARCO. It's on, man.

RUCKUS. Marco, this fryer is not on. Do I need to re-train you? We open in ten minutes.

MARCO. We open in an hour.

RUCKUS. Well, I figured out we can make like six hundred extra bucks a week if we open early, and we won't tell my dad. We can just pocket the cash.

MARCO. If your dad doesn't know we're open, how does anyone else know we're open, Genius?

RUCKUS. Watch it or you're gonna be wearing a chicken costume screaming at cars on the street, fucking *telling* everyone we're open.

MARCO. I'd get shot.

RUCKUS. Damn right you'd get shot. I'd shoot you. And I'd get away with it too. I'd be like, "I'm sorry, Officer, but there was this crazy chicken out on the street just squawking and running around, it was fucking huge. And it's my right to carry a weapon."

MARCO. Not yet.

RUCKUS. Age is a technicality, Marco. You gotta learn to finesse the system. See, I've got finesse. You've got a job at a Dougal's earning minimum wage.

MARCO. So do you.

RUCKUS. But I'm the manager. I make twenty-five cents more than you. Per hour. Seriously, man, what's wrong with you?

MARCO. Nothing.

RUCKUS. The fryer isn't heating.

MARCO. It'll heat. Leave it alone.

RUCKUS. Did you see the guy get shot or something?

MARCO. Nah.

RUCKUS. Then what are you all freaked about?

MARCO. There was blood all over the road.

RUCKUS. That's what happens when people get shot.

MARCO. You're such a psycho.

RUCKUS. I'm not a psycho, I just understand the facts.

MARCO. You're one of those trench coat kids. You're gonna come to school one day and kill everyone.

RUCKUS. No way, man. I love school. We're reading *Great Expectations.* That book's a laugh-riot. I have great expectations that it's gonna have a great ending that I never expected.

MARCO. Are we smoking or what?

RUCKUS. You're the one who's about to shit themselves about Emma smelling it.

MARCO. She's always late.

RUCKUS. So, she'll be late today.

MARCO. You scared the shit out of her last time.

RUCKUS. That's what a manager does. She was breaking company policy. Crime and Punishment, yo.

MARCO. You might want to get a brain scan, you could be retarded. They can figure that shit out with tests these days.

RUCKUS. Yeah. I guess I'd rather not know.

MARCO. You're an idiot.

(**RUCKUS** *pulls a bag of pot out of his backpack. Throughout the following, he meticulously rolls a joint.*)

RUCKUS. I'm a doctor, man. I'm a fucking faith healer.

MARCO. Whatever, just roll it.

RUCKUS. Don't rush it.

MARCO. If she yells at us, you're telling her I didn't smoke.

RUCKUS. Who cares if she yells at us? I'm the boss.

MARCO. You're an idiot.

RUCKUS. You're just jealous.

MARCO. Listen, Ruckus, can you cover for me at lock-up? My sister's sick and my mom wants me to pick up her meds before curfew.

RUCKUS. Marco. You have made a commitment to Dougal's. There is supply and demand here. I supply you with a job so you can buy a new bike or a dildo or whatever it is you're fucking after and I *demand* that you work the full day.

MARCO. You suck.

(**RUCKUS** *lights the joint and they smoke it.*)

RUCKUS. So you see any body parts or just the blood?

MARCO. Fuck you.

RUCKUS. No, I'm serious. Come on, man, you can leave early.

MARCO. It wasn't just one guy, it was a bunch of guys. They tried to pull over a Hum-V and the driver freaked. A bunch of guys got out of the car shooting and tried to cross like six lanes of traffic. They got most of them. A couple got away, I think. A bunch of people got shot.

RUCKUS. You saw this happen?

MARCO. Nah. That's just what I heard.

RUCKUS. Fuck, man. I can't wait to turn eighteen.

MARCO. All the fighting'll be over by the time you're eighteen. They'll have you typing up the general's screenplay.

RUCKUS. What are you talking about?

MARCO. It's almost over now.

RUCKUS. How do you know?

MARCO. My stepdad.

RUCKUS. Steve? The guy with the comb-over who lives in your house? Like he tells you anything.

MARCO. He says the fighting's almost over. He says it's a matter of weeks.

RUCKUS. I don't think so.

MARCO. We'll see, I guess. My stepdad's in the fucking military and your dad owns a Dougal's but you should tell me more about what you know.

RUCKUS. Don't smart-mouth your boss, Marco. Where the fuck did you hide my hat?

MARCO. I didn't hide anything.

RUCKUS. You hid it because you know Emma loves power. And you thought she'd see me in my manager hat and have to have me, like right on the floor in front of you and you would have to watch. And then you'd be embarrassed of your boner 'cause you're hot for me.

MARCO. I didn't hide your hat.

RUCKUS. You really think the fighting's almost over?

MARCO. That's what he said.

RUCKUS. But they've been saying that for like three years.

MARCO. Steve says soon.

RUCKUS. What does Steve know?

MARCO. More than you do.

RUCKUS. Fuck that. I got two months.

MARCO. He says it's a matter of weeks.

RUCKUS. Fuck that.

MARCO. What do you want a gun so badly for?

RUCKUS. *Uh*, to kill people. To look at. To stroke.

MARCO. They'll have you taping up windows.

RUCKUS. Dude, I would be pulling people over and shooting them on the highway. Like bam, I just killed you, you fucking traitor.

MARCO. Sometimes I'm afraid of you, man.

RUCKUS. You should be. I'm scary.

(The door opens and **EMMA** *enters. She is seventeen years old, wearing her Dougal's uniform and a pair of white sneakers with pink laces.)*

RUCKUS. *(imitating a porn soundtrack)* Bow-chicka-wah-wah.

EMMA. Hey, Marco.

MARCO. Hey, Emma.

RUCKUS. Nothing for me?

EMMA. Hi, Colin

RUCKUS. That's not my name.

EMMA. You guys have been smoking, haven't you? You fucking douchebags.

RUCKUS. Emma. I'm the manager now, so you might want to watch what you say to me.

EMMA. Fuck you, Ruckus. The fryer isn't even on. What have you guys been doing?

RUCKUS. See, Marco?

MARCO. I turned it on.

EMMA. It's not hot.

MARCO. Give it a minute.

EMMA. You guys are a total waste of space. I'm the only one who ever does anything around here.

(She pulls a hat out of the fryer.)

Who left their hat in the fryer? This is why it's not heating, you're jamming the tube.

RUCKUS. That's my fucking hat.

EMMA. Great job, Ruckus. It melted.

RUCKUS. I didn't leave it there.

EMMA. You could've started a fire.

RUCKUS. Well, good thing I didn't leave it there.

EMMA. You actually made manager. You cock.

RUCKUS. You impressed?

EMMA. No.

RUCKUS. *(to* **MARCO***)* She's impressed.

EMMA. Fucking nepotism. You guys see the news? They got a bunch of guys on the highway.

RUCKUS. Marco was a witness.

EMMA. Really?

MARCO. Nah. I was just caught in traffic.

RUCKUS. Bullshit, Marco. You saw the blood.

EMMA. You did?

MARCO. Well, it was all over the road.

EMMA. My mom made me drive around it.

RUCKUS. Marco got off his bike and went to go check it out.

EMMA. Did you see anything?

MARCO. I didn't even stop.

RUCKUS. Shut up, dude. You can tell her.

MARCO. I didn't...

RUCKUS. He got off the bike and started walking towards it. It was one of those huge Hum-V's and people were saying to get back 'cause there were people with guns but fucking Marco, man, he's got balls.

MARCO. Ruckus.

RUCKUS. Like big fucking balls. Like watermelons or those decorative balls you buy at Pier One hanging off the side of his dick. It's like bam, balls, swinging like a pendulum fucking hitting him in the leg when he walks. Anyway—

MARCO. Shut up, dude.

RUCKUS. Don't be modest, Marco. You've got a captive audience.

EMMA. Ruckus, leave him alone.

RUCKUS. Anyway, he's walking down the side of the highway. He's got to be careful, right? 'Cause there are fucking people with guns, but none of them's got balls as big as Marco's, so he keeps going.

EMMA. Stop talking about his balls.

MARCO. Thank you.

RUCKUS. So then he sees it. There's this guy in the middle of the road and he's bleeding, right? He's bleeding all over the place. He's got these huge popped-out eyes and his head is cracked, like maybe he got shot, Marco doesn't know, he's just fucking standing there looking at this guy.

EMMA. So who was it?

RUCKUS. Who the fuck do you think it was?

EMMA. A soldier?

RUCKUS. Not one of ours.

EMMA. How did you know?

RUCKUS. He just knew. He could feel it in his big psychic balls.

EMMA. So what'd you do?

RUCKUS. He looked the guy right in the eyes, stared him down. And then he killed him.

MARCO. No I didn't.

RUCKUS. Shut up, Marco.

EMMA. This is total bullshit, this story.

RUCKUS. No way, man. He knelt down and he put his fingers around the guy's neck and strangled him 'til his eyes popped all the way out and he turned blue. It was the only humane thing to do at that point.

EMMA. No way.

RUCKUS. Yes way.

MARCO. I didn't do that.

RUCKUS. Marco's so modest. Modest Marco.

MARCO. I'm not modest. I didn't kill anyone.

RUCKUS. People started running out from all directions looking for the guy, 'cause it turned out he was the baddest motherfucker of them all.

EMMA. Shut up, Ruckus.

RUCKUS. Modest Marco just waits there next to this guy's corpse until all the soldiers arrive. When they get there they are all like totally psyched 'cause, like I said, this guy was bad. People are interviewing him and shit, and he's all, "Oh it's no big thing, I did it for my country." And then some guy from MTV asks him if they could do a reality show about what it's like to have huge nuts.

MARCO. That didn't happen.

EMMA. Ruckus. You're a douche.

RUCKUS. Whatever. Marco's being modest, he can be modest. But he's getting honored in some secret government ceremony. He asked if he could get off work early today to get there. He's gotta catch a train, and he's gotta get there early to get an extra seat for his humongous balls.

EMMA. Turn the fryer on Ruckus.

MARCO. You're such an asshole, you know that? Sometimes you're such an asshole.

RUCKUS. Marco, the truth will set you free.

EMMA. Did anyone turn on the speaker in the drive thru?

MARCO. I'll do it.

EMMA. What do you guys do when you get here? You have a circle jerk and then sit around smoking pot?

RUCKUS. There aren't really enough people for a circle jerk.

EMMA. Whatever. I'm turning on the speaker, and when I come back, you two better have the fryer situation figured out or I'm calling your dad.

RUCKUS. Yeah right.

EMMA. Just do it. Please.

MARCO. We'll do it.

RUCKUS. Since you asked nicely.

(**EMMA** *hops the counter and exits through the front door to turn the speaker on.* **MARCO** *stares at* **RUCKUS**.)

RUCKUS. Why are you looking at me like that?

MARCO. That didn't happen.

RUCKUS. Look, man, if you want people to pay attention to you, you gotta give them a reason to be interested in you. Seriously. I did you a favor.

MARCO. Great.

RUCKUS. Oh come on, dude, she doesn't think you killed anyone. Have you met yourself? You're a pussy.

MARCO. What if she told someone?

RUCKUS. Oh shit, wouldn't that be terrible? People might actually respect you. Come on, man, at least she's interested.

MARCO. No she isn't.

RUCKUS. Yes, Marco, she is. Trust me, I know a lot more about this shit than you do. Now fucking turn the fryers on before something really shitty happens to you, like I kill you.

MARCO. Okay. Fine.

(**MARCO** *moves to turn the fryers on.*)

(*There is a large blast outside. It comes out of nowhere and reverberates around the room.*)

MARCO. What the fuck was that?

RUCKUS. I don't know.

(*Emma returns.*)

EMMA. What was that?

RUCKUS. You see anything?

EMMA. There's smoke everywhere.

MARCO. *(at the window)* Jesus.

EMMA. I gotta call my mom.

RUCKUS. Your mom lives in the woods. She's fine.

EMMA. I'm calling her.

(*The lights begin to flicker – we hear the roar of airplanes overhead.*)

RUCKUS. You think it's a strike?

MARCO. I don't know.

RUCKUS. Chill out, dude. Nobody's blowing up a Dougal's.

MARCO. It sounds close.

RUCKUS. No shit.

EMMA. My phone's not working.

(**MARCO** *moves to pull the blackout curtains. All of a sudden, the door to the Dougal's swings open, and a* **MAN** *staggers in. He is bloodied and obviously very hurt. He can barely stand up on his own.*)

(*The three kids look at him.*)

(*The* **MAN** *staggers and then falls. Another large blast shakes the room. This time the blast is closer.*)

Scene Two

(Seconds later. One of the lights is flickering, a window is broken.)

(Through the window we can see the neon "D" of the Dougal's sign hanging off the side of the roof. **EMMA,** **MARCO,** *and* **RUCKUS** *stand over the* **MAN.** *He is passed out.)*

RUCKUS. Emma get the mop. We need to clean this place up before any customers get here.

EMMA. Who is this guy?

RUCKUS. I don't know. Get his wallet.

(No one moves.)

MARCO. You get his fucking wallet.

RUCKUS. Fine.

*(**RUCKUS** opens the **MAN**'s coat.)*

No wallet.

EMMA. Maybe it's in his car or something.

*(**RUCKUS** runs to the window.)*

RUCKUS. No cars in the lot except my Jeep and Emma's piece of shit.

EMMA. Shut up, Ruckus.

MARCO. He walked here.

EMMA. Nobody walks here.

RUCKUS. Jesus.

EMMA. What?

RUCKUS. Jesus fuck.

EMMA. What?

(beat)

Ruckus, what?

RUCKUS. Who do you know that walks these roads?

EMMA. He could just be a guy.

RUCKUS. Look at him.

MARCO. You think everyone's a traitor.

EMMA. We should call the police.

RUCKUS. What are they gonna do about it?

EMMA. Come get him.

RUCKUS. Look out the window. They might have more important things to deal with.

MARCO. I'll call my stepdad.

RUCKUS. We can handle this.

EMMA. Handle what? What is there to handle?

RUCKUS. Open his shirt, Marco.

MARCO. Why? No.

RUCKUS. Just fucking do it. He could have a bomb strapped to his chest.

MARCO. No way.

RUCKUS. You're a pussy, dude.

MARCO. You do it.

EMMA. Don't touch him, Ruckus.

RUCKUS. Both of you need to shut up.

(**RUCKUS** *gets down next to the* **MAN** *and starts searching his pockets. He opens his shirt. His hands come back bloody.*)

RUCKUS. Jesus, look at this guy.

EMMA. I am freaking out. I am totally freaking out.

RUCKUS. Marco, get some rope.

MARCO. Rope? What are you talking about?

RUCKUS. You want this guy to wake up and shoot us in the fucking head?

MARCO. You just searched him. He doesn't have a gun.

RUCKUS. If he's one of them, he's trained. He could probably kill us with a spatula. Get some rope.

MARCO. We don't have any rope. Why would we have rope?

RUCKUS. I've got rope in my car.

MARCO. Of course you have rope in your car.

(**MARCO** *exits in search of rope.*)

EMMA. He needs to go to a hospital, Ruckus, he's bleeding everywhere.

RUCKUS. It'll be an hour wait for an ambulance. St. Vincent's got hit last week.

EMMA. Then we'll drive him.

RUCKUS. I'm not getting in a car with that guy.

EMMA. Ruckus, we have to do something.

RUCKUS. If you want to go outside in the middle of a strike, be my guest, but there's no way I'm getting blown up today.

EMMA. I'm calling the hospital.

RUCKUS. Fine.

(**EMMA** *pulls out her cell phone and starts dialing.* **MARCO** *comes back with rope.*)

RUCKUS. Tie his feet.

MARCO. Together?

RUCKUS. Yes together, you fucking moron.

MARCO. Sorry. I don't spend a lot of time tying people up.

EMMA. It's not dialing. There's no signal.

RUCKUS. Everyone's trying to call out.

MARCO. Try the other phone.

(**EMMA** *picks up the restaurant phone.*)

EMMA. It's dead.

RUCKUS. See?

EMMA. What are you gonna do with him?

RUCKUS. Just shut up and let me think.

MARCO. There are, like, twenty-five health code violations right here.

RUCKUS. Tie his legs.

(**MARCO** *moves toward the* **MAN** *with the rope. The* **MAN** *moves slightly, groaning.*)

MARCO. What the fuck, the guy just moved. I swear to God, he moved.

EMMA. He's moving.

RUCKUS. Yeah I saw it.

MARCO. What am I supposed to do? The guy's fucking moving.

EMMA. He's moving, Ruckus.

RUCKUS. I can see that, you guys.

EMMA. What should we do?

RUCKUS. Hit him.

MARCO. What?

RUCKUS. Hit him, Marco. Knock him out.

MARCO. I'm not hitting this fucking guy.

RUCKUS. Just do it.

MARCO. You do it.

RUCKUS. Do I have to do everything?

MARCO. You're the psychopath. We just want to call the cops.

RUCKUS. The phones are dead, you jackass.

MARCO. I'll go out to the station. I'll ride there.

RUCKUS. And leave us here two on one? Or like one and a half on one since Emma's a girl.

EMMA. Fuck you.

RUCKUS. Just hit the guy before I hit you.

MARCO. No way.

RUCKUS. Fine.

(**RUCKUS** *picks up a frying pan lying on the counter and approaches the* **MAN** *cautiously. Suddenly, the* **MAN** *moves. Everyone screams.* **RUCKUS** *hits him harder than he probably meant to.*)

(*The* **MAN** *falls back on the floor.*)

EMMA. Jesus Christ.

RUCKUS. Tie his legs.

MARCO. Ruckus, you killed him.

EMMA. He killed him?

RUCKUS. I didn't kill him.

(**MARCO** *moves over to the* **MAN** *and ties his legs.* **EMMA** *fights back tears.*)

RUCKUS. What are you crying about?

EMMA. I'm not crying.

RUCKUS. Emma. Don't cry.

EMMA. I'm not fucking crying.

(**RUCKUS** *stands up and walks over to her.*)

Maybe he's just some guy on the way to some kid's soccer game. Maybe he just got in a car crash.

RUCKUS. Look, we'll find out who he is, okay? And if we made a mistake, I'll apologize.

EMMA. He could just be some guy.

RUCKUS. He got shot, Emma. He's bleeding from his leg, okay? People don't get shot at their kid's soccer game. Take a look.

EMMA. Okay. I get it.

RUCKUS. Let's just get him in the storeroom and when the phone lines are free we'll get help. Emma, grab his legs please.

EMMA. No. I'm not a part of this.

RUCKUS. You are a part of this.

EMMA. No, I'm not. I didn't even touch him. You hit him with a frying pan, Marco tied his legs, I didn't touch him.

RUCKUS. You watched.

EMMA. I gotta find my mom, she could've gotten hurt.

RUCKUS. She's not hurt. She's reading a magazine in your living room right now. She's letting her nail polish dry.

EMMA. You don't know.

RUCKUS. Emma. Please. We open in a half hour.

MARCO. We can't open.

RUCKUS. We're opening.

EMMA. Ruckus, we can't open.

RUCKUS. We have to open. My dad'll kill me. Just grab his legs and help me and Marco pull him into the storeroom.

EMMA. No.

RUCKUS. Then get the goddamn door.

(**RUCKUS** *and* **MARCO** *grab the* **MAN**'s *arms and legs and start dragging him in.*)

(**EMMA** *opens the door and* **RUCKUS** *and* **MARCO** *drag the* **MAN** *into the storeroom. It is a difficult process. The lights fade as they are struggling to get him inside the door.*)

Scene Three

(The storeroom.)

(A lamp hangs from the ceiling, a couple of lockers, a ratty couch, beat-up Playstation, etc.)

(As the lights come up, the **MAN**, *who we will now call* **LOUIS**, *is tied to a chair. A shirt is wrapped tightly around his leg, soaked in blood.)*

(He looks around, trying to figure out where he is. He begins to realize just how much pain he is in.)

*(***MARCO*** is sitting on the couch, staring at him.)*

MARCO. You're awake.

LOUIS. Who are you?

MARCO. Marco.

LOUIS. Who?

MARCO. Who are you?

LOUIS. Louis. What am I doing here?

MARCO. I'm supposed to tell him when you're awake.

LOUIS. Tell who?

MARCO. Ruckus.

LOUIS. Who?

MARCO. Colin Rucker. He's the manager.

LOUIS. The manager of what?

MARCO. I'm not supposed to tell you anything.

LOUIS. How old are you?

MARCO. Don't ask me any more questions.

LOUIS. I'm bleeding pretty bad, Kid.

MARCO. We tied that shirt to your leg to stop the bleeding.

LOUIS. It hasn't stopped, Kid. Look at my leg.

MARCO. Don't call me Kid.

LOUIS. How did I get here?

MARCO. I have to tell him you're awake. I would tell him the truth if I were you.

LOUIS. Who?

MARCO. Ruckus.

LOUIS. Please, Marco. Take a look at my leg. I need help.

MARCO. Sorry, man.

(**MARCO** *exits.*)

(**LOUIS** *looks around the room. He looks down at his leg, which has stopped bleeding for the moment, but looks terrible. The shirt tied around it is completely soaked in blood.*)

(*A moment later the door opens and* **RUCKUS** *enters.* **LOUIS** *looks at him – another kid?*)

LOUIS. Are you Ruckus?

(**RUCKUS** *stares him down.*)

LOUIS. *(cont'd)* Look, Kid, I'm bleeding pretty bad. I gotta get out of here, get this checked out. Kid? You don't really want to watch me die here, do you?

RUCKUS. What's your name?

LOUIS. Louis.

RUCKUS. What is that, French?

LOUIS. No.

RUCKUS. Louis. Is that your real name?

LOUIS. Yes, that's my real name.

RUCKUS. Okay.

LOUIS. What?

RUCKUS. Okay, that's fine.

LOUIS. Who do you think I am?

RUCKUS. Who shot you?

LOUIS. I don't know.

RUCKUS. You don't know.

LOUIS. There was a lot of confusion. People screaming and shooting.

RUCKUS. So. You weren't at your son's soccer game.

LOUIS. What?

RUCKUS. Just answer the question.

LOUIS. I don't have kids.

RUCKUS. So somebody shot you, you didn't see who.

LOUIS. How old are you?

RUCKUS. What are you doing here?

LOUIS. I'm tied up.

RUCKUS. You came to us.

LOUIS. Us?

RUCKUS. Me, Marco and Emma.

LOUIS. Emma?

RUCKUS. She's won't come in here. She's scared of you.

LOUIS. Why would she be scared of me?

RUCKUS. No one's gonna find you, Louis.

LOUIS. Did I walk here?

RUCKUS. So you better talk.

LOUIS. Why am I tied up?

RUCKUS. Why wouldn't you know who shot you?

LOUIS. Where am I?

RUCKUS. There are a lot of questions, I guess. Right, Louis?

LOUIS. This is a mistake.

RUCKUS. Did you hear the news this morning? Thirty-three people dead on the highway. A bunch of guys jumped out of a Hum-V and started shooting.

LOUIS. No, I didn't hear that.

RUCKUS. Two got away.

LOUIS. Okay.

RUCKUS. Where were you this morning?

LOUIS. You think I was one of those guys?

RUCKUS. I don't know what I think yet.

LOUIS. I wasn't in that car.

RUCKUS. It was a Hum-V.

LOUIS. Okay. I wasn't there.

RUCKUS. Wanna know something crazy?

(beat)

Well, do you?

LOUIS. Okay.

RUCKUS. I found out my history teacher has been spying on students. You ever hear of something like that? A *professional* teacher spying on his students? Seeing if any of us have ties. You know?

LOUIS. That's terrible.

RUCKUS. Lucky for me, I don't have any ties.

(*beat*)

What are you doing in New Jersey?

LOUIS. I forget to bring my passport or something?

RUCKUS. You know anyone here?

LOUIS. I got an aunt who lives here.

RUCKUS. An aunt.

LOUIS. Yeah, my aunt lives in South Orange.

RUCKUS. Oh. Is that so. What's her name?

LOUIS. Aunt Cathy.

RUCKUS. Aunt Cathy. I could look her up?

LOUIS. Sure.

RUCKUS. What's her last name?

LOUIS. Garrison.

RUCKUS. I'll have one of them look into it.

LOUIS. The thing is, she's out of town a lot. Since it started. She's scared all the time. Lives alone.

RUCKUS. Oh.

LOUIS. I'm saying, call her, but if she's not there, she's just out of town a lot.

RUCKUS. So you think we won't be able to reach her.

LOUIS. I'm not saying that, I'm just saying—

RUCKUS. You don't have an aunt Cathy who lives in New Jersey.

LOUIS. I do. Cathy Garrison. My mom's sister. Call her.

RUCKUS. I will.

(*beat*)

Who are you running from?

LOUIS. I can't run. Have you seen my leg?

RUCKUS. That's funny. You're funny, Louis.

LOUIS. Look, kid, I need a doctor or I'm gonna lose this leg.

RUCKUS. You know they're looking for you, right? It might not be too smart to see a doctor right now.

LOUIS. Who's looking for me?

RUCKUS. Everyone. You're a wanted man, Louis.

LOUIS. You made a mistake.

RUCKUS. Do you want a cigarette, Louis?

LOUIS. No.

RUCKUS. That kid out there – Marco – you remember him?

LOUIS. What about him?

RUCKUS. He was there on the highway this morning. He saw it go down, okay? He saw the bodies. He recognizes you.

LOUIS. What?

RUCKUS. He saw you. He described you. In detail. So I'd say you're fucked.

LOUIS. What are you trying to do, Kid?

RUCKUS. If you call me Kid one more time, I'm gonna kick you in that fucking leg.

LOUIS. Okay. I'm sorry.

RUCKUS. I just want to know who you are.

LOUIS. I'm Louis. My last name is Griffin. I'm from Connecticut. I'm thirty. What else? I live in Bridgeport with my girlfriend, Sarah. We have a dog.

RUCKUS. What kind of dog?

LOUIS. A poodle.

RUCKUS. You have a poodle?

LOUIS. It's hers.

RUCKUS. I don't believe you have a poodle.

LOUIS. I do.

RUCKUS. Well that's pretty gay, man.

LOUIS. I'm sorry.

RUCKUS. You live with your girlfriend and a poodle.

LOUIS. Yes.

RUCKUS. You think I'm stupid?

LOUIS. No.

RUCKUS. I'm aware of how these things work, okay?

LOUIS. What things?

RUCKUS. What?

LOUIS. How what things work? You're aware of how what things work?

RUCKUS. You want a cigarette, Louis?

LOUIS. No. I don't want a cigarette.

RUCKUS. You don't smoke?

LOUIS. I'm in a lot of pain here.

RUCKUS. I'm sorry about that.

LOUIS. I need a doctor.

RUCKUS. Honestly, Louis, I would seriously advise against that.

LOUIS. Have you ever seen a person bleed to death?

RUCKUS. You trying to scare me, Louis?

LOUIS. Why am I tied to this chair?

RUCKUS. Sure you don't want a cigarette, Louis?

LOUIS. Yes, I'm fucking sure. What are you gonna do to me?

RUCKUS. I gotta consort with my colleagues.

(**RUCKUS** *pulls a bandana around* **LOUIS**' *mouth - a makeshift gag.*)

LOUIS. Hey! What are you doing? I can't breathe!

RUCKUS. I'll be back. Don't go anywhere.

LOUIS. Hey! Hey!

Scene Four

(**EMMA** *is sitting on the drive-thru stool at the drive-thru
window. She has a headset resting around her shoulders.*
MARCO *sits on the floor.* **RUCKUS** *bursts through the
door.*)

RUCKUS. He's lying.

MARCO. Can't we just let him go, man?

RUCKUS. Let him go?

EMMA. What if he bleeds to death? None of us will go to
college.

RUCKUS. So we just let him go.

MARCO. We're just saying, maybe we should think about—

RUCKUS. Listen, you let that guy go, he's gonna go get his
guys and they're gonna come to our houses tonight
and they're gonna shoot us in the head. Or maybe he
blows up the rest of the Empire State Building, and we
have to know that we coulda stopped it. You want to
live the rest of your life knowing that?

EMMA. No, but—

RUCKUS. But on the other hand, let's say we keep him
around. Let's say we even find out who he is and what
he's doing here. We'll be heroes. Someone'll make a
movie about us.

EMMA. I don't care, Ruckus. My mom won't care about a
movie.

RUCKUS. She'll care if you're dead, you moron.

MARCO. Ruckus, cut it out.

RUCKUS. We're not letting the guy go. I'm the manager
and I'm managing this situation. I'm surprised at you,
Marco, seriously, after the kind of shit you've been
through.

MARCO. Leave me alone.

RUCKUS. Emma, look up a Cathy Garrison in South
Orange.

EMMA. Why?

RUCKUS. He says she's his aunt.

EMMA. What am I supposed to say to her?

RUCKUS. You're not gonna talk to her, dumbass, the phones aren't even working.

MARCO. Ruckus, I swear to God.

RUCKUS. I just want to know if there is a Cathy Garrison in South Orange.

(**EMMA** *pulls a phone book out from under the cash register. She thumbs through it. It takes a second.*)

RUCKUS. It's under G.

EMMA. I know.

RUCKUS. Just making sure.

EMMA. Fuck you.

RUCKUS. Ouch.

MARCO. Leave her alone, man.

RUCKUS. Marco, watch your boner, I don't want you to split your uniform.

MARCO. Bite me.

EMMA. There's no Cathy Garrison. There's a Beth Garrison and a Carol and Steve Garrison. No Cathy.

RUCKUS. There's his first lie.

MARCO. Maybe she's unlisted.

RUCKUS. He told me to look her up.

EMMA. Why would he lie about that?

RUCKUS. 'Cause he doesn't know anyone in Jersey. Or if he does, he doesn't want us to know them.

EMMA. You really think he's—

RUCKUS. Yes, Emma, I really do.

EMMA. This is so fucked up. I can't get involved in this.

RUCKUS. Are you kidding? Write your college essay on this shit – you'll go to Harvard.

EMMA. Oh, OK Ruckus. I'll write my college essay about the time me and two stoners tied some guy to a chair in the back room of a fucking Dougal's while his leg bled out all over the floor. Great. I'll write about that. Thanks.

RUCKUS. It should be the homeless shelter you worked at instead of a Dougal's. Colleges are more impressed by homeless shelters.

EMMA. I'm gonna kill you, Colin. I'm serious.

(She storms off into the employee bathroom.)

MARCO. Just leave her out of it.

RUCKUS. If you think she's gonna fuck you, Marco, you are sorely mistaken.

MARCO. She's just scared.

RUCKUS. You know what your problem is, man? You're a floater. You're like a smart kid or whatever but you don't do anything about it. You don't ever try to improve your situation.

MARCO. The guy's bleeding—

RUCKUS. You gotta think a little, Marco. You don't think. You're gonna be one of those guys who wakes up one day and looks in the mirror and thinks, "Fuck. I'm fat, old and bald." And then you'll just lie back down and count the seconds 'til you die. Now when I wake up fat, old and bald, should that day ever come – I'll stand up, go outside, fucking go for a run. Shoot a rabbit. Skin it. Put it on my bald ass head and go to Hooters.

MARCO. Skin a rabbit?

RUCKUS. Yeah, a fucking rabbit. Or like a squirrel.

MARCO. That's disgusting.

RUCKUS. That's disgusting.

MARCO. I'm just saying.

RUCKUS. I'm surprised at you, Marco.

MARCO. Shut up, man.

RUCKUS. I'm not trying to hurt your feelings, man, but you're acting like this doesn't affect you, like you couldn't care less about what's going on. But you don't get a choice. You have to care. That douchebag in there coulda been the one who got your dad.

MARCO. You don't know what you're talking about.

RUCKUS. Oh come on, Marco. You think he's eating raspberries and watching Dr. Phil in some fucking camp?

MARCO. One of these days, man, I'm gonna kill you—

RUCKUS. Listen. I told the guy you recognize him.

MARCO. You told him what?

RUCKUS. I told him you were there this morning and you recognize him.

MARCO. I don't recognize him.

RUCKUS. Yeah, man, but he's scared. He thinks you do.

MARCO. But what if he wasn't there?

RUCKUS. He was there.

> *(beat)*

Look, you do whatever you want. I told the guy you recognize him. You can blow my cover if you want, make me lose my credibility, or you can help me take this guy down.

MARCO. Take him down?

RUCKUS. You know, figure out who he is?

MARCO. You think he believes you?

RUCKUS. What does he know? He doesn't even remember how he got here.

MARCO. I'm bad at lying.

RUCKUS. Bullshit.

MARCO. I am.

RUCKUS. What about when you told Jessica Danna that she had "oceanic" eyes? That girl did not have "oceanic" eyes, my friend. She *was* oceanic. As in like, as big as a fucking ocean.

MARCO. Just don't blame me if he figures it out.

RUCKUS. Try your best, man. Give it your all. Go for the gold.

MARCO. Just don't be such an asshole to Emma.

RUCKUS. Well, you're in luck, man, because I'm not an asshole, I'm a fucking prince.

MARCO. Just don't say anything to her.

RUCKUS. I could ask her to blow you.

MARCO. Fuck you.

(*MARCO exits into the men's bathroom.*)

(*RUCKUS starts rummaging around the room looking for something. He picks up a frying pan, swings it a little, puts it down. Then he moves over to an eggbeater and wields it like a sword, miming hitting someone with it. He carefully tests the weight of each item and mimes hitting someone with it, figuring out which one will be his weapon of choice.*)

(*EMMA enters. She watches him for a second.*)

EMMA. What are you doing?

RUCKUS. Hey, welcome back to the party.

EMMA. (*about* **MARCO**) Is he okay?

RUCKUS. He's taking a shit.

EMMA. What did you say to him?

RUCKUS. Nothing.

EMMA. Don't be so hard on him, okay?

RUCKUS. God you guys are perfect for each other. "Don't be so hard on him." "Go easy on her."

EMMA. He said that?

RUCKUS. Yeah, he gave me a big lecture about how to treat women.

EMMA. Well, did you listen?

RUCKUS. Um, no. I'm sorry, but I don't take girl advice from Marco. I apologize if that seems crazy to you.

EMMA. You should be nicer to him. He likes you. I bet there aren't that many people who do.

RUCKUS. Oh, wow. Cold. I am nice to him.

EMMA. Yeah.

RUCKUS. I'm talking about making Marco a man, okay? Giving him a chance to take some responsibility for himself.

EMMA. You shouldn't talk about his dad.

RUCKUS. He's a pussy. He'll feel better if he grows a pair.

EMMA. Just leave his dad alone, okay? He doesn't want to talk about it.

RUCKUS. So, what? You're gonna start dating him now? Marco? Are you serious?

EMMA. Shut up. I'm leaving, okay?

RUCKUS. No you're not.

EMMA. Yes I am. I'm leaving. I don't want any part of this. My mom would kill me if she knew what we were doing. I have to make sure she's okay, and I'm leaving. Dock my pay, I don't give a shit.

RUCKUS. Emma, you can't leave.

EMMA. Oh, what? You're gonna stop me?

RUCKUS. He's seen your face, Emma. He knows what you look like.

EMMA. No he doesn't.

RUCKUS. He asked Marco about you.

EMMA. No he didn't.

RUCKUS. He did. He asked about the girl.

EMMA. He's just some guy, Ruckus. And you're going to jail. And I'm not gonna stick around just so I can go too.

RUCKUS. I just don't want anything to happen to you. I know Marco would jump out a window if anything happened to you. And Marco's the only person who knows how to fix the toilet, so this is really a business decision.

(A long beat.)

EMMA. Let me talk to him, then. Let me talk to the guy.

RUCKUS. Why?

EMMA. 'Cause I'm the only one who's got an IQ above ten.

RUCKUS. What are you gonna say to him?

EMMA. Whatever I want to say to him. I don't answer to you.

RUCKUS. Don't untie him.

EMMA. I'm not gonna untie him. But if I have to stay here, then I get to talk to him. That's just the way this is gonna work

RUCKUS. Alright. You talk to him. You ask him about Cathy Garrison in South Orange. You ask him why he lied. Hey, you might even be able to help. Women have incredible instincts, psychic tits or whatever.

EMMA. Okay, Colin.

RUCKUS. Not my name.

(**MARCO** *re-enters.*)

MARCO. What's going on?

RUCKUS. Emma's gonna talk to the guy.

MARCO. What? Why?

EMMA. You don't think I can handle it?

MARCO. No, I do, I just—

EMMA. You scared for me, Marco?

MARCO. I just didn't think you wanted to—

EMMA. Well, Ruckus won't let me leave so I thought I'd help out.

MARCO. You want me to come in with you?

EMMA. No.

MARCO. I'll be right outside, okay? If you need me.

EMMA. Sure, whatever, Marco.

(**EMMA** *exits into the storeroom.* **RUCKUS** *looks at* **MARCO.**)

RUCKUS. (*imitating him*) I'll be right outside, okay? If you need me.

MARCO. Shut up.

RUCKUS. You remember that time we were at Six Flags and those girls were in front of us in line? They had those little tube tops on, with their bathing suits underneath, and their suits were all wet so they had those huge wet boob stains?

MARCO. What did you say to her?

RUCKUS. And they were talking the whole time they were in line about how scared they were to go on the roller-coaster. They kept saying it over and over again. And we were laughing at them, 'cause it was so obvious they wanted us to talk to them. "Oh, I'm so scared of the roller-coaster. Oops, I dropped my corndog. Oh wow, I can't believe how big my tits are!" And finally, you told that one girl, Tiffany, that you would ride with her?

MARCO. Yeah. I remember.

RUCKUS. It was at that moment, man, that I fell in love with you. Come on. You're a pimp when you want to be.

Scene Five

(The storeroom.)

*(***EMMA*** *stands behind* ***LOUIS****' chair, afraid to move any closer.)*

LOUIS. Hello?

*(***EMMA*** *stays still.)*

Ruckus?

EMMA. Hi.

LOUIS. Emma?

EMMA. How do you know my name?

LOUIS. They keep talking about you.

EMMA. Great.

LOUIS. I'm not going to hurt you. You can come closer if you want.

EMMA. Okay.

*(***EMMA*** *moves closer to* ***LOUIS*** *so that he can see her.)*

LOUIS. Hi.

EMMA. I'm sorry you're tied up.

LOUIS. Yeah, me too.

EMMA. I told them not to do it, but they were scared.

LOUIS. I'm gonna lose my leg.

EMMA. No you're not. Come on, I'll help you.

LOUIS. How?

EMMA. You gotta know that I'm not with them, okay? Like if anyone asks? I'm on the record, this is a shitty idea.

LOUIS. Okay. Tell them to let me go.

EMMA. They won't listen. I can try to get you a doctor.

LOUIS. I just need to get out of here.

EMMA. The phones are down, but the army's got a temporary med base a couple miles from here and if I take my car I think I can get one of the doctors to come back with me.

LOUIS. Just untie me and I'll go there myself.

EMMA. You can't walk. You won't make it there.

LOUIS. I can walk. Just let me go.

EMMA. What are you so afraid of?

LOUIS. Your friend's gonna kill me.

EMMA. Okay, let me tell you something about Ruckus. He talks a big game but like, he could never kill you. He's too stupid.

LOUIS. Well, that's reassuring.

EMMA. Just let me get you a doctor and you'll be OK.

LOUIS. That kid is gonna hurt me. Just help me get out of here and you'll never see me again.

EMMA. What? You're not from around here?

LOUIS. Emma.

EMMA. Where are you from?

LOUIS. Bridgeport.

EMMA. Oh. How do you like it there? I've never been there.

LOUIS. It's nice.

EMMA. Cool. So you don't want a doctor 'cause they're looking for you?

LOUIS. Nobody's looking for me.

EMMA. Or maybe you just don't want an army doctor. The army's definitely looking for you.

LOUIS. No one is looking for me.

EMMA. So I should believe you.

LOUIS. I'm telling the truth. I promise.

EMMA. Nobody tells the truth.

LOUIS. No, I'm just – My name is Louis.

EMMA. I don't care what your name is.

LOUIS. Please don't do this.

EMMA. I was trying to help you. Your leg is bleeding all over the floor.

LOUIS. You have to untie me.

EMMA. You just hit the city, right? You didn't hit any of these towns, right?

LOUIS. I don't know what you're talking about. I'm just trying to get home. I have a baby.

EMMA. You what?

LOUIS. I have a baby.

EMMA. What kind of baby?

LOUIS. What?

EMMA. Boy or girl?

LOUIS. A girl. She's six months old. I told the other kid, I told Ruckus I didn't have any kids – I was scared he would try to use that against me. But I do, I have a daughter.

EMMA. I don't believe you.

LOUIS. Her name is Bella.

EMMA. Bella. Like *Twilight?*

LOUIS. Catherine Bella.

EMMA. You're lying.

LOUIS. I'm not lying.

EMMA. Did you tell me that 'cause I'm a girl? 'Cause like, I'm into babies and ponies and shit? So I'll feel bad for you?

LOUIS. No, I just—

EMMA. My mom would kill me if she knew what I was doing right now. She barely leaves her bedroom anymore. She's scared of everything. This morning she took a shower with all her clothes on. Like she was afraid she'd have to leave at any moment. She wanted to make sure she was dressed.

LOUIS. I'm sorry.

EMMA. Some bad stuff has happened to her, okay? And you think I'm just gonna let you go?

LOUIS. I just want to disappear.

EMMA. I'm sorry, man, you walked into the wrong restaurant.

LOUIS. I know your boyfriend thinks I'm one of them.

EMMA. Which one of them's my boyfriend?

LOUIS. Ruckus?

EMMA. Wrong.

LOUIS. Do you want to be here to watch me die? You want to watch me bleed to death?

EMMA. I was trying to help you.

LOUIS. I'm not who they say I am.

EMMA. My mom and I, we used to have this neighbor, this French guy, Ralph. I think he might have been dating my mom but I don't really know, I was still too young to know about that kind of stuff. Anyway, they were really close. He would have dinner at our house all the time – he would bring me stuff from France – snow globes, postcards, things like that – and he made my mom pretty happy. When he was around, she wasn't scared, you know? She was sleeping through the night. I think she liked knowing he was next door. But then one day he was just gone. He just stopped calling us or coming over. And after about a week, my mom sent me over to his house to check up on him, make sure he was okay, but he was gone. His house was empty. He didn't call or leave a note or anything. He just left. And then a couple days later, France turned and then there was that huge air strike – something like ten thousand people. So we figured he got a call telling him to leave. But he could have told us. He could have warned us.

LOUIS. Why are you telling me this?

EMMA. It's hard to keep everyone straight these days. It's hard to tell who's good.

LOUIS. I'm going to die here.

EMMA. You're not gonna die.

LOUIS. I'm gonna lose my leg.

EMMA. Well, that's your own fault.

LOUIS. Fine, please get me a doctor. I want a doctor.

EMMA. Who shot you?

LOUIS. I don't know.

EMMA. If you just talk to me, I can help you. They'll listen to me.

LOUIS. This is a Dougal's, right? I recognize the uniforms.

EMMA. If you talk to me, I can help you.

LOUIS. I don't know what you want me to say.

(*The door opens and* **RUCKUS** *and* **MARCO** *enter.*)

RUCKUS. What's going on in here?

EMMA. I offered to get him a doctor, but he says he doesn't want one.

LOUIS. I didn't say that.

EMMA. And he says he's got a daughter named Bella.

LOUIS. Emma, please.

RUCKUS. You told me you didn't have any kids.

LOUIS. I have a daughter. I thought you would use that against me.

RUCKUS. Well, you lied. I'll probably use *that* against you.

LOUIS. I didn't lie, I was just trying to protect myself.

RUCKUS. There's no Cathy Garrison in South Orange. How do you explain that?

LOUIS. My aunt lives in South Orange. She probably took her number out of the phone book. I told you, she's scared all the time.

MARCO. Who are you?

LOUIS. I'm just trying to get home to my family.

RUCKUS. What's your real name?

(*Suddenly, a voice begins to crackle over the drive-thru speaker.*)

VOICE. (*O.S.*) Hello? Hello?

(**RUCKUS,** **EMMA,** *and* **MARCO** *look at each other.* **LOUIS** *begins to scream. Ad lib as the teenagers try to shut* **LOUIS** *up.*)

RUCKUS. Shut up.

LOUIS. Help me!

RUCKUS. Shut the fuck up, Louis!

EMMA. What do we do?

LOUIS. Ahhhhhh! Help!

>   (**RUCKUS** *hits* **LOUIS**. *Hard.* **LOUIS** *is knocked out.*)

EMMA. Oh my God.

VOICE. *(O.S.)* Is anyone there? Hello? Can I place an order please? Hello?

RUCKUS. Emma. Go take her order.

EMMA. Should we—

RUCKUS. Go take her order.

EMMA. I—

RUCKUS. Go take her order.

>   (**EMMA** *runs into the other room.* **RUCKUS** *and* **MARCO** *look at each other and at* **LOUIS** *' body slumped over in the chair.*)

>   (*From the other room we can hear:*)

EMMA. Hi there. Welcome to Dougal's. Can I take your order?

>   *(beat)*

Hello? Hello?

Scene Six

(The storeroom. **LOUIS** *is still tied.* **RUCKUS** *stands over him.)*

RUCKUS. I used to have this friend, Louis. You would have loved this guy, he would do anything. His name was John but everyone called him Pepper – to this day I seriously have no idea why, but it was fitting, okay? 'Cause this guy sort of made you want to sneeze. Like he was a little bit sleazy, but it was a good thing for him. It sort of worked for him.

Anyway he basically invented fruit bongs at our school. I don't know if you've ever smoked out of an apple or whatever, but it's nice. It gets you high and there's this sort of apple-y taste that you don't really expect and it hits you in this really nice way, makes you happy. You feel like you're drinking apple juice – it's like fifth grade only it's drugs. Anyway, Pepper got people started on other fruits, like melons. Pineapples, sometimes smaller things like pears or plums, whatever. So the point is, people liked him. He was always a good guy to have around – he made people relax. Whatever, you didn't mess with him.

But then in, I don't know, ninth grade, Pepper starts to get squirrely. He's all itchy in class, you know, like panicked. He starts sweating all the time which everyone agrees is gross, but no one wants to say it to his face because up until this point, the dude's like the king of the school.

Fine, whatever. We deal.

But then, Pepper starts asking questions. Like weird fucking questions that no dude would want to know. Questions about our parents and what they think of the government, things like that. Questions we don't know the fucking answers to, 'cause like, we don't care. Fine whatever, we give Pepper the benefit of the doubt, 'cause we've got history with the dude.

But then, shit starts to get weird. Pepper starts digging. And I mean digging.

The dude is in my fucking house going through my drawers when I'm in the bathroom. He's always around and he's looking for shit on me. On all of us. Not just me. Everyone.

At parties, it's the same old Pepper. He's fun, smoking out of fruit, telling jokes, throwing girls in the pool, whatever. But when it's one-on-one you're kind of scared, right? You're starting to get scared because you're thinking, *shit, what have I told this guy?* 'Cause this dude knows everything about us, like right from the fucking beginning – like Kindergarten, man, I'm not kidding. So we figure we gotta hold a meeting. Right? We have to 'cause this guy is about to sell our secrets. And I don't even know what these secrets include at this point, maybe nothing, maybe something. I've done some crazy shit and I've got friends who have parents in the military, shit like that. People who should be protected.

So we call a meeting. This girl Lauren's house. And we all get there, but guess who else is there? You got it – Pepper. And he's all, "You guys having a party?" So we're thinking, now that's fucking weird, he's got our phones tapped. The kid was always really good with computers and shit. So finally, I confront him. Everyone decides that someone needs to do it and they pick me, 'cause I'm not really afraid of Pepper and most of the rest of the kids at school are, 'cause the dude is fucking scary. Sure, he could be cool, but you didn't want to catch him alone in an alley, you know?

The point is: he's working for the enemy. The motherfucker is on the other side, working for the enemy – giving them info about our parents, about us. He's gotten secrets about military stuff from those kids who know extra shit 'cause their dads are involved. It's not a ton of stuff, but it's stuff, you get it? He stands there in my room and just tells me, to my face, just like that, "I'm working for them," like it's something to be proud of. Like I should be jealous. The whole time he's got this big smile on his face.

And I'm wondering why Pepper would turn like that. Doesn't he remember the beginning? But he's involved now. He's one of them.

We had a fight. I broke the kid's nose, which I genuinely felt bad about at the time. I told him we were through as friends, which he was okay with – I mean, he had to know it was coming. He didn't come to school the next day or ever again, which was good for him, 'cause everybody knew he had turned. I felt bad for breaking the kid's nose, I really did. I wasn't violent, I just felt strongly. I was ignorant then. I think about it now and I'm angry. 'Cause if I ever saw that kid again, I swear I'd kill him. I wouldn't even think twice. I think you know what I'm getting at, Louis.

LOUIS. I have no idea what you're getting at.

RUCKUS. How old are you, man?

LOUIS. Twenty-eight.

RUCKUS. Okay. So you still remember what it's like to have friends. You have any friends, Louis?

LOUIS. Yes. I have friends.

RUCKUS. And you'd do things for them, right? You know what loyalty is, right?

LOUIS. Yes. I know what loyalty is.

RUCKUS. I'm a loyal bastard, Louis. That's a secret about me. I put on this tough façade but inside I'm like a little fucking puppy – loyal to the end. I try not to get too attached to people, because when I do, I start getting really scared about the kind of things I would do for them. You know?

LOUIS. No I don't know.

RUCKUS. I think you do.

LOUIS. No I don't.

RUCKUS. I think you know that I'm about to get mean.
That you better start telling the truth or things are
gonna get kind of bad for you.

LOUIS. You're just a kid, man. What are you getting yourself
into?

RUCKUS. You don't want to know what I'm capable of,
Louis. In two months, I'll be fighting. You have no
idea what I'm capable of.

*(We hear the sound of airplanes, like rumbling thunder
overhead.)*

Those your friends?

LOUIS. I'm not who you think I am.

RUCKUS. But you're not who you said you are either.

(We hear the sound of an explosion in the distance.)

Scene Seven

*(Front of the restaurant. The lights are flickering and the sound of planes continue. **EMMA** is dialing her cell phone. **MARCO** paces the floor.)*

EMMA. I have to get out of here.

MARCO. We're safe here.

EMMA. I need to call my mom. Jesus Christ.

(to her phone)

Work, you bitch.

MARCO. He's been in there a long time.

EMMA. My phone's still not working.

MARCO. What do you think he's doing? Do you think the guy's talking?

EMMA. I don't know, Marco. How should I know?

MARCO. Sorry.

(beat)

You know, those strikes are pretty routine. My stepdad says they try not to hit any civilian targets – that means schools, hospitals—

EMMA. I know what it means.

MARCO. Well, anyway, they're probably just going for army bases and things like that.

EMMA. What about your stepdad?

MARCO. He'll be okay.

EMMA. My mom didn't even want me working. She's scared I'm gonna get shot every time I go out.

MARCO. But you're okay. I'll make sure you get home tonight.

EMMA. You think I could get a Sprite?

MARCO. Yeah. Sure.

EMMA. Ruckus would say no.

MARCO. Well, he's not here.

EMMA. I can't believe he made manager. I've seen him spit in people's Cokes before. I mean the guy has the IQ of a cheeseburger. His brain is made of ham.

(**MARCO** *hands her a Sprite.*)

Thanks.

MARCO. If he comes back in, you should hide that.

EMMA. Don't listen to him, okay?

MARCO. Who, Ruckus? I don't.

EMMA. I know he's been saying shit about your dad.

MARCO. It's fine. I don't listen.

(*changing the subject*)

My stepdad says it's almost over.

EMMA. How does he know?

MARCO. He hears rumors, I guess.

EMMA. What does that mean?

MARCO. Surrendering maybe. Or a cease-fire.

EMMA. Surrendering?

MARCO. I don't know. If it comes to that.

EMMA. Jesus.

MARCO. It would be okay. Better than this.

EMMA. My mom got called up.

MARCO. What?

EMMA. Yeah. I don't think they'll let her hold a gun. She's got nails out to here.

MARCO. Wow. I'm sorry.

EMMA. It just really sucks.

MARCO. I'm sorry, Emma.

EMMA. I mean, I guess it's good news it's almost over, right?

(*They sit in silence for a moment.*)

Ruckus probably tells you that I'm into him.

MARCO. Aren't you?

EMMA. He's a loser, Marco. He's cool now because he has a car. He wants everyone to think he's tough, so all he wants to do is fight people. It's not an attractive quality.

MARCO. Oh.

EMMA. It's not like I'm sitting around looking for boyfriends.

MARCO. I didn't think you were.

EMMA. You just shouldn't listen to everything he says all the time. A lot of the time, he's totally off-base. Like about me, for instance.

MARCO. What about you?

EMMA. You're so thick.

MARCO. What?

EMMA. You don't even know how to flirt, Marco.

MARCO. What are you talking about?

EMMA. Nothing.

MARCO. I know how to flirt.

EMMA. Right. Okay.

MARCO. What? Are you flirting with me?

EMMA. Me?

MARCO. Never mind.

EMMA. I'm joking. Yes. I'm flirting with you, Marco. Don't be such a doofus. Thanks for the Sprite.

(During the following dialogue, we begin to see the action between **RUCKUS** *and* **LOUIS** *in the storeroom.)*

RUCKUS *rips a large piece of duct tape and places it over* **LOUIS**' *mouth. He punches* **LOUIS** *in the face – hard.)*

EMMA. What was that?

MARCO. I don't know.

*(***EMMA** *moves to the door.)*

EMMA. Ruckus? Everything okay in there?

(From inside, **RUCKUS** *replies:)*

RUCKUS. Fine. Just stay out there.

(**EMMA** *moves away from the door.*)

EMMA. Ugh. You know I made out with him once?

MARCO. Yeah. I know.

EMMA. He told you?

MARCO. He told a bunch of us – like a bus full of people.

EMMA. Great.

MARCO. No, I mean, 'cause he was proud of it.

EMMA. He's a really bad kisser.

MARCO. Yeah?

EMMA. Yeah, I mean, he's okay. He uses his teeth a lot which is gross. Kind of clanky. Plus he still had braces at the time.

(**RUCKUS** *snaps a stapler in* **LOUIS**' *face and then staples the fleshy part of his ear.*)

MARCO. Do you want some more Sprite?

EMMA. I'm good.

MARCO. Okay.

EMMA. But thank you.

MARCO. No problem.

(**RUCKUS** *kicks* **LOUIS** *in the leg.* **LOUIS** *doubles over in pain.*)

(*There is a silence between* **MARCO** *and* **EMMA.** **MARCO** *looks anxiously at the door.*)

EMMA. What am I gonna do when my mom has to report?

MARCO. When's she been called for?

EMMA. I don't know, two or three weeks. I'm still in school. What am I supposed to do?

MARCO. They have programs.

EMMA. Yeah right. I'm not living in some bunker.

MARCO. You could stay at my house. I'm sure my mom would—

EMMA. That's nice, Marco. It's okay.

MARCO. Okay, but the offer's on the table. So if you want—

(**RUCKUS** *chokes* **LOUIS** *with the chord of a Playstation controller.*)

EMMA. What if something happens to her?

MARCO. Nothing's gonna happen. You said yourself, she won't be holding a gun.

EMMA. I thought she was too old.

MARCO. Well, they need bodies. People, I mean.

EMMA. My friend, Miranda, she's got a sister who remembers what it was like before. I don't remember anything.

MARCO. I do.

EMMA. You do?

MARCO. Well, I remember my dad, I guess.

EMMA. Sorry I brought it up.

MARCO. Nah, it's okay.

(*A moment.*)

EMMA. Are you angry?

MARCO. All the time.

EMMA. You don't ever seem angry.

(*They look at each other.*)

You want to kiss me or something?

MARCO. What?

EMMA. You were looking at me like you want to kiss me.

MARCO. I was–

EMMA. You can, you know. And you don't always have to wait until someone says it's okay. Sometimes you can surprise people.

MARCO. Okay. Well, I won't let you know when it's gonna be then.

EMMA. So you *are* gonna kiss me?

MARCO. I'm sorry but that information's classified.

(**EMMA** *laughs.* **MARCO** *kisses her. It is sweet and brief. They kiss again, and this time it lingers. They pull away.*)

EMMA. I'm sorry you're so angry.

*(***RUCKUS*** *bends down close to* **LOUIS** *' leg wound and jabs it with a pen.* **LOUIS** *screams.* **EMMA** *and* **MARCO** *rush to the door.)*

EMMA. What the hell was that?

MARCO. Ruckus? What's going on in there?

(The door re-opens and **RUCKUS** *enters with blood on his hands.)*

EMMA. Jesus, is that blood?

MARCO. What did you do?

RUCKUS. *(to* **EMMA***)* Is that a Sprite?

MARCO. I bought it for her.

EMMA. Jesus, Ruckus, what did you do to him?

RUCKUS. I talked to him. Hand me that towel.

*(***EMMA*** *hands* **RUCKUS** *a dishrag.)*

(The door to the Dougal's opens and a young man, about twenty-two enters. They freeze. Let's call him **PAUL***. He walks up to the counter.)*

PAUL. Hey. Do you work here?

RUCKUS. Yeah. What's up?

PAUL. My car stalled. You think maybe I could get a burger and a jump?

RUCKUS. Sure. Emma, help this guy out. I'm on break.

*(***EMMA*** *walks to the counter as* **RUCKUS** *exits to the bathroom, hiding his bloodied hands.)*

EMMA. Hi.

PAUL. Hi.

EMMA. What can I get you?

PAUL. You're supposed to say "Welcome to Dougal's."

EMMA. Welcome to Dougal's.

PAUL. Don't worry. I won't tell on you.

EMMA. Okay.

PAUL. I used to work here.

EMMA. Cool.

PAUL. The place looks exactly the same. What up? I'm Paul.

EMMA. Hi.

PAUL. What's your name?

EMMA. Emma.

PAUL. How long you been working here?

EMMA. A year.

PAUL. Who's the quiet guy?

MARCO. I'm Marco.

PAUL. *(about the broken Dougal's sign)* Hey man. What happened to the D?

EMMA. Air strike.

PAUL. Fuckin' crazy, right? You guys go to Madison?

MARCO. Yeah.

PAUL. I went to Madison. You guys know Billy Porter? He's my best friend's little brother. Tall kid, sort of fat. He makes a really stupid face sometimes. It's like, "bloob!" He used to make that a lot when he was a kid.

EMMA. Sorry. I don't know him.

PAUL. I probably know a bunch of people there. What year are you?

EMMA. What can I get you?

PAUL. Geeze, no chatting. Your boss here or something?

EMMA. No, I'm just reorganizing the closet.

PAUL. Oh man, closet duty. That sucked. We always made the new kid do it. Hazing. But it was sort of fun. Can I come on back? Look at the place? I haven't been back in a while.

EMMA. We're not actually allowed to let people back here.

PAUL. Okay, chill. I just wanted to take a look around. I wrote my name in the...

(He gestures toward the back room.)

– just wanted to see if it's still there.

MARCO. They repainted everything.

PAUL. Bummer. You guys have any customers today?

MARCO. Nah.

EMMA. What's it like out there?

PAUL. Air strikes.

MARCO. How many people?

PAUL. I don't know, three hundred maybe.

MARCO. Jesus.

PAUL. It's a good day. Either of you guys got jumper cables?

MARCO. We keep a pair in the back. I can get 'em.

PAUL. Thanks. I can't believe my car stalled in the middle of an air strike. You should've seen me on the road, I was freaking out, trying to hide in a ditch.

MARCO. I'll be right back.

(**MARCO** *exits into the storeroom.*)

EMMA. Where's your car?

PAUL. About a half a mile down the road.

EMMA. How'd you get here?

PAUL. I walked.

EMMA. Did you get shot at?

PAUL. You're like a detective.

EMMA. Sorry. What can I get you?

PAUL. You know, I was the manager when I was here.

EMMA. Cool.

PAUL. A cheeseburger, I guess. What's good here now?

EMMA. Whatever you want.

PAUL. Alright, alright. A cheeseburger. Meat. Cheese. Old school.

EMMA. You want fries?

PAUL. Nah. They're no good here. I always thought they tasted like fingers. Not that I know what fingers taste like? I've never eaten fingers.

(*beat*)

They caught those guys. So that's a good thing.

EMMA. What?

PAUL. The ones from the highway this morning – the two that got away. Those guys are in fucking trouble. I wish I could see their faces, you know, like "oops."

EMMA. When did they catch them?

PAUL. I don't know, couple hours ago. I was watching the news, my brother's stationed in DC so I was checking in on things over there. But yup, they caught the guys – they were trying to hide in the Lincoln Tunnel. Couple of soldiers nabbed 'em.

Killed one of them, the other one's getting locked up.

EMMA. Wow.

(beat)

PAUL. Hey, sure I can't just come on back and say hi to the old place? I'm pretty sure I left some weed in one of the lockers.

EMMA. I'm sorry. The manager would freak.

PAUL. Come on, just a quick look around.

EMMA. Here's your burger.

PAUL. Alright, I get it.

EMMA. Two fifty

PAUL. Steep.

*(**MARCO** returns.)*

MARCO. I got the cables.

PAUL. So is he the manager?

EMMA. Nah. The manager's in the bathroom.

PAUL. Oh that guy?

MARCO. Yeah. His dad owns the place.

PAUL. Well that sucks. You guys'll never make manager.

MARCO. It's okay.

EMMA. You want to jump your car now?

PAUL. She's all business, huh?

MARCO. Yeah, I guess so.

PAUL. I don't know whether I should go out just yet with the strike and all. Maybe I'll stay here, eat my burger and then I'll go.

MARCO. Okay.

EMMA. What kind of car do you have?

PAUL. A Honda.

EMMA. What model?

PAUL. Nancy Drew and the Cheeseburger Caper.

EMMA. I just like cars is all. How long did it take you to get here?

PAUL. Ten minutes. I ran.

EMMA. What do you want?

PAUL. What do you mean?

EMMA. What do you want from us?

PAUL. Man, a guy asks for a cheeseburger and look what happens–

MARCO. Emma.

EMMA. He didn't walk here. He would've gotten shot. It would have been safer to stay in the car –

PAUL. What are you saying? I'm lying to you?

EMMA. Yeah, I think you're lying.

PAUL. Why would I do that?

EMMA. I don't know. You tell me.

MARCO. Emma.

EMMA. Get Ruckus.

MARCO. Emma, don't do this. Let's just give the guy the cables – let him jump the car. You got a car you can jump it with?

PAUL. It's okay, guy, the girl's right. You can't trust anybody.

EMMA. Why do you want to come back here so badly?

PAUL. I used to work here. Why don't you want me to come back there?

EMMA. 'Cause I'll get in trouble.

PAUL. What are you hiding?

EMMA. Nothing.

PAUL. You know, you could get in a lot of trouble if you're hiding something.

EMMA. I don't think so.

PAUL. You don't think so? You don't think I have any authority to get you in trouble? Maybe I just happen to tell someone that you've got something hiding back there.

EMMA. It's a health code violation.

PAUL. Or someone? Maybe you got *someone* hiding back there.

EMMA. I don't have a hair-net for you.

PAUL. Maybe you're offering refuge to the enemy. That kind of thing could get you killed.

EMMA. You're not authorized to be back here.

PAUL. I think maybe I'll check it out for myself.

EMMA. No you won't.

PAUL. You're gonna stop me?

EMMA. That's right.

MARCO. Emma, hold on.

(*calling into the other room*)

Ruckus!

(**PAUL** *moves toward the back of the restaurant.* **EMMA** *picks up a frying pan.*)

PAUL. What are you nuts? You're gonna hit me with that? I'm gonna get killed by some fast food waitress with a frying pan?

EMMA. Don't take another step.

PAUL. You've got a guy back there, don't you?

EMMA. Marco.

(**PAUL** *takes another step and* **EMMA** *swings at him and misses.*)

PAUL. You missed.

EMMA. Don't come any closer.

PAUL. Trust me, kid, don't make this any harder than it has to be. I'm just gonna take a look around. I'm looking for someone who might have come by this way – did you see anyone?

EMMA. No. Stay back.

PAUL. I think you've seen someone. In fact, I think you've got him back there. You can get in a lot of trouble for hiding people in times like these. You didn't think people would be looking for him?

EMMA. Looking for who? What are you talking about?

PAUL. *(calling)* Louis! I know you're here!

(PAUL pushes EMMA aside as she swings at him with the frying pan. MARCO lunges at PAUL, pushing him into the fryer. PAUL lands headfirst in hot grease. Screaming and clutching his face, he falls to the floor. EMMA, terrified, keeps kicking him. He passes out.)

(MARCO looks on, frozen with terror.)

(RUCKUS enters.)

RUCKUS. Jesus Christ. What happened here?

(EMMA turns on RUCKUS.)

EMMA. You asshole.

(She begins hitting him with her fists.)

RUCKUS. What the hell? Stop it.

EMMA. They found those guys from the highway. They caught them. Both of them. Now I killed this guy.

MARCO. He's not dead.

RUCKUS. Who is he?

MARCO. He was looking for Louis. He said he could get us in trouble.

RUCKUS. Easy on the trigger finger, Emma.

EMMA. I didn't know what to do – he was gonna find out.

RUCKUS. Grab his legs.

EMMA. Are you listening? They found those guys from the highway.

RUCKUS. Then why was he looking for Louis?

MARCO. I don't know.

EMMA. That means he wasn't there.

RUCKUS. It doesn't mean anything. At this rate, we're bringing down the whole fucking enemy by dinner rush.

EMMA. He wasn't one of those guys.

(**RUCKUS** and **MARCO** begin moving **PAUL**'s body.)

Scene Eight

(The storeroom. **LOUIS** *looks terrible. His face is a mess. His eye is turning black and blue and he can barely keep his head up.)*

*(***PAUL*** *is now tied up and passed out on the floor of the storeroom.)*

*(***EMMA*** *stares at* **LOUIS**. *She is holding a glass of water and some napkins.)*

EMMA. What did he do to you?

(no response from **LOUIS***)*

He hit you pretty bad, huh?

(no response)

EMMA. You don't have to talk to me. But I could help you.

*(***LOUIS*** *lifts his head up and struggles to speak.)*

LOUIS. Who is that?

EMMA. Just a guy.

LOUIS. Collecting bodies?

EMMA. You tell me who he is.

LOUIS. I've never seen him before.

EMMA. He was looking for you.

LOUIS. He doesn't look very good.

EMMA. I brought you some advil.

LOUIS. Advil.

(beat)

What did Ruckus do to you?

LOUIS. What does it look like?.

EMMA. Why didn't you just tell him what he wanted to hear?

LOUIS. I don't know what that is. Who is this guy?

EMMA. Who shot you?

LOUIS. What happened to his face?

EMMA. I don't think you're one of them.

LOUIS. That's 'cause I'm not.

EMMA. But you could be. What do I know? I've made mistakes about that kind of thing before. Sometimes people are really convincing. Who is this guy?

LOUIS. I don't know.

EMMA. He said he thought we might be hiding someone. He said your name, said he was looking for you.

LOUIS. You have to let me go, Emma.

EMMA. I can't let you go, okay? I don't know you. You seem nice, but you could just kill me. Without me, my mom would...I just can't do that, okay? So stop asking. Besides, Ruckus would fire me.

LOUIS. He would fire you.

EMMA. Yeah, he's really serious about this shit.

LOUIS. If I stay here they'll find me. That guy, he'll wake up.

EMMA. Who is he?

LOUIS. I can't go back there.

EMMA. Who are you running from?

LOUIS. *(beat)* Is that water for me?

EMMA. You want some?

LOUIS. Please.

EMMA. Then you'll talk to me.

(**EMMA** *moves toward* **LOUIS** *with the water. She puts it to his lips. He grabs her wrist and pushes her to the ground.*)

LOUIS. Don't scream. If you scream, I'll break your arm. Untie my legs.

EMMA. You're hurting me.

(**EMMA** *unties his legs.* **LOUIS** *stands feebly.*)

LOUIS. Now sit down.

EMMA. Why?

LOUIS. Sit in the chair.

EMMA. What are you gonna do?

> (**LOUIS** *grabs a pair of scissors out of a cup on the*
> *microwave. Every movement is fluid, as if he has been*
> *planning this move since the moment he woke up in that*
> *room. He grabs* **EMMA** *and pushes the scissors toward*
> *her neck. She sits.*)

LOUIS. You're going to help me get out of here. Get up.
Open the door.

> (**LOUIS** *pushes* **EMMA** *into the kitchen.*)

Scene Nine

LOUIS *pushes* EMMA *into the kitchen holding the scissors to her neck.*

RUCKUS. What are you doing, man?

LOUIS. Give me one of your cars.

RUCKUS. Fuck no.

EMMA. Ruckus.

RUCKUS. You can give him your piece of shit, Emma, but my dad's car's a fucking Jeep.

LOUIS. I've got a pair of scissors to her neck.

RUCKUS. You know they found those guys from the highway.

(beat)

RUCKUS. Yeah. So I guess we made a mistake. I guess you're just some guy. We were gonna let you go, Louis.

MARCO. Louis, please, just let her go.

RUCKUS. But I don't think we're going to do that now.

EMMA. Ruckus.

LOUIS. In ten seconds, I will dig these scissors into her neck. They will cut through the artery and blood will start spilling onto her chest. It will make a gurgling sound like running water. And then I'll dig them in a little deeper and I'll cut through the wind pipe and air will start escaping. That will sound like a balloon deflating. And then she will die. And you will have to watch her die. I'm not the kind of person who wants to watch someone die, but I know how to make it happen. Ten. Nine. Eight.

(In a fit of adrenaline, MARCO *rushes at* LOUIS, *knocking him to the ground.* EMMA's *rushes to* RUCKUS.)*

*(*MARCO *punches* LOUIS *as hard as he can, over and over again, pummeling him into the ground.* LOUIS, *whose strength left him long ago, lies on the ground, taking it.)*

(Finally after a long and violent moment, **RUCKUS** *pulls* **MARCO** *off of* **LOUIS**. **LOUIS** *lies beaten on the ground.)*

RUCKUS. Calm down, man.

MARCO. *(muttering, transfixed, surprised at his own strength)* Sorry. Sorry. Sorry. I'm sorry.

LOUIS. I'm gonna die in a Dougal's.

EMMA. Marco.

RUCKUS. You having fun yet, Louis? Anyone want to apologize for doubting me?

EMMA. Marco, are you okay?

RUCKUS. Are we all prepared to admit that I've been right this whole time? Marco?

*(**MARCO** stares at **LOUIS**, fixated.)*

EMMA. Marco.

MARCO. I didn't mean to.

Scene Ten

(The lights come up on the storeroom. **PAUL** *groans.* **RUCKUS** *kicks him, causing* **PAUL** *to pass out again.* **LOUIS** *sits on the chair.* **RUCKUS** *sits down on a chair looking at* **LOUIS.** **MARCO** *stands in a corner.)*

RUCKUS. My dad owns this place, you know.

LOUIS. Wow.

RUCKUS. Yeah, he bought it a couple years ago. He used to be in real estate. He thought about selling now all the fighting's moving north, but people have stopped buying in New Jersey. More people leaving than coming.

LOUIS. That makes sense.

RUCKUS. I'm the manager.

LOUIS. Wow.

LOUIS. What are you, sixteen?

RUCKUS. I'll be eighteen in two months.

LOUIS. And then you're joining.

RUCKUS. Can't wait. Marco will tell you. Tell him, Marco.

MARCO. He can't wait.

LOUIS. What about you, Marco?

*(***MARCO*** *doesn't respond.)*

LOUIS. Or are you just the quiet kid in the corner who beats the shit out of people?

MARCO. You almost killed her.

LOUIS. You don't know what's out there. It's like a monster and it's moving toward you. It's got legs. You look out your window one night and it's far off in the distance. And then you wake up one day and it's in your backyard. You'll wake up one morning and New York will be gone.

RUCKUS. You saying you know something? You know if I see something, I gotta say something.

LOUIS. When this thing started, I was twenty. That was eight years ago.

RUCKUS. Just tell us what you know.

LOUIS. I don't know anything. What am I supposed to know?

RUCKUS. You said we'll wake up one morning and New York will be gone – what does that mean? What the fuck does that mean, Louis?

LOUIS. I don't know what it means. It's the pain talking.

RUCKUS. Tell me what it fucking means or I swear to God, I'll—

LOUIS. You'll what? Kill me?

RUCKUS. Maybe I will.

LOUIS. Go ahead.

RUCKUS. Maybe I will.

LOUIS. So go ahead.

*(**EMMA** enters.)*

EMMA. What's going on?

LOUIS. Your friend's gonna kill me.

EMMA. What?

RUCKUS. Go back out there and watch the door.

LOUIS. Go ahead, Emma. Do what you're told.

MARCO. It's okay. Nothing's gonna happen.

*(**EMMA** turns and exits.)*

LOUIS. Oh, so you're her boyfriend. I thought she had a thing for your friend.

RUCKUS. Well, I'm kind of a lone wolf.

LOUIS. *(about **PAUL** tied on the floor)* You know, he's not gonna let this go.

RUCKUS. So you do know who he is.

LOUIS. I can take a guess.

RUCKUS. Would you care to share? Do I need to pass you the talking stick?

LOUIS. He thinks you're protecting me.

MARCO. Why would we protect you?

LOUIS. Come on, you don't have to be tough. I know you're scared. So am I. When I volunteered, they told me I'd be stationed up here, far away from the action – when it was over, I could go back to school. They needed people, it was supposed to be a summer thing. But that was eight years ago. And no one volunteers anymore.

RUCKUS. So you *are* a soldier.

LOUIS. So now you're fucked, aren't you? Now you're thinking *maybe he's one of us.*

MARCO. Are you?

LOUIS. You go to sleep at night and hope to God you'll wake up in the morning. You hear the planes flying over your head and you just hope they keep on going. And then one night, you won't hear them. But you'll know they're there. You'll know they're there, cause you can't hear them.

RUCKUS. Who are you?

LOUIS. They told me it was gonna be a summer thing.

MARCO. What are you doing here?

LOUIS. I'm just trying to disappear, Kid. I know you don't want to fight. You're right not to want to fight. You'd be smart if you dug yourself a hole and stayed down there 'til this was all over.

MARCO. You ran away?

LOUIS. I've done my duty, okay? I've done it three times over. And now it's time for me to get out while I'm still alive.

MARCO. You just left people out there. People died because of you.

LOUIS. You don't know what you're talking about.

MARCO. You're a fucking coward.

LOUIS. You don't know what you're talking about.

RUCKUS. Watch what you say, Louis.

MARCO. My dad was in Virginia, stationed outside of D.C. to stop the approach. He was in a team of fifteen men. They were at a weigh-station on the highway, keeping lookout, just waiting. Two days before, they escaped from a blast, a couple of guys got killed. And so they were resting. Fifteen guys from all over the place. Friends.

In the middle of the night, my dad wakes up and he's alone. He and two other guys are alone there. The rest of them ran off. Didn't tell my dad or anybody. And they took the guns with them. They left one gun for three guys. Or that's the story they told us. Where do you think he is now, Louis? I don't know. Maybe you know. Do you know, you fucking coward? It's people like you—

LOUIS. I'm sure your dad was terrified.

RUCKUS. Louis, you're a real sensitive guy. Marco, did I tell you this guy's got a poodle?

MARCO. When we tell them you're here, you'll have to go back. They'll destroy you.

RUCKUS. Do you know what happens to deserters, Louis?

MARCO. They'll destroy you.

RUCKUS. I told you, Marco. Didn't I say this? Right from the fucking beginning I said this coulda been the guy.

MARCO. Shut the fuck up, Ruckus.

RUCKUS. Dude, I'm on your side.

LOUIS. Let me explain. Please—

MARCO. I don't want to hear anything you have to say.

LOUIS. I can explain...

MARCO. I could kill you, man. I could kill you and not feel bad about it.

RUCKUS. Modest Marco grows a pair.

MARCO. Shut the fuck up, Colin.

RUCKUS. That's not my name.

LOUIS. Listen, Kid, I—

MARCO. Don't call me kid. I'm not a kid okay?

LOUIS. I'd rather die than go back there.

RUCKUS. Be careful what you wish for.

LOUIS. Do it then!

RUCKUS. Marco, this guy just cordially invited you to kill him.

(*MARCO turns on* **RUCKUS** *with an anger we've never seen in him before.*)

MARCO. I swear to God, man. Just shut the fuck up or I will rip your throat out.

RUCKUS. Jesus.

MARCO. No, I'm serious, Ruckus. You're a fucking loser. You're a loser, man, and you're never gonna not be one.

RUCKUS. Marco, not in front of the guy.

MARCO. Just shut up, man, for one second. I told you I didn't want this. I said it over and over again.

RUCKUS. Okay, sorry.

LOUIS. Guys..

RUCKUS. Shut up.

LOUIS. I can't get a word in, can I?

MARCO. Shut up! Just shut the fuck up!

(*MARCO exits, slamming the door.* **RUCKUS** *is stunned. A long beat.*)

LOUIS. You're not a loser.

RUCKUS. I kind of am. It's cool. It works for me.

LOUIS. You can do something good here.

RUCKUS. I'm not your friend, man.

(**RUCKUS,** *embarrassed, ashamed, exits before* **LOUIS** *can see him cry.* **EMMA** *enters and stands looking at* **LOUIS.**)

EMMA. Is everything okay?

RUCKUS. Ask that fucking deserter.

(**EMMA** *goes into the storeroom.*)

LOUIS. Are you gonna watch him kill me?

(about **PAUL***)*

That guy, he's paid to find deserters. Do you know what he'll do to me when he wakes up?

EMMA. You'll take your punishment and then you'll go back to wherever you came from.

LOUIS. They'll kill me. They'll drag me into the street. They'll do it together.

EMMA. You're just scared.

LOUIS. You can't know what makes a person run until you're running.

EMMA. My mom got called up. She's leaving in a couple weeks.

LOUIS. I'm sorry.

EMMA. People keep deserting. They just keep calling people up. I don't have anybody else.

LOUIS. You think it's over but it's not. It's coming.

EMMA. What is?

LOUIS. Every day it's coming closer.

EMMA. What is?

LOUIS. This morning, we pulled over a Hum-V. Inside it were six men. Supposedly big names on the list – we have a list of names, people we kill without asking questions.

The guys got out of the car and started shooting and running down the highway. Two got away. I don't know how 'cause there were bullets everywhere – both sides shooting. A bunch of civilians got in the way and we just shot them – it doesn't matter, right? 'Cause these were people we needed—

EMMA. I don't want to hear this.

LOUIS. Please listen. Meanwhile, the enemy's got a couple thousand guys lined up waiting for our guys to move to the highway toward the Hum-V, to take the bait. These six guys were a decoy. Probably some kids, your age, maybe, told close to nothing, sent to die.

And I start looking around and I realize that I'm going to get killed if I stay here. They'll send me in some car to get killed, they'll use me as bait. There are bodies in the Lincoln Tunnel. People shooting each other – no one knows who's who, everyone looks the same.

Those guys, the bad guys, they're running like clowns all over the freeway getting shot by soldiers and by people in their cars. Moms getting out of minivans with pistols, shooting these boys down in the middle of a five lane highway.

And all of a sudden, I realize I'm running. I can't even feel it, my legs are moving without me. I'm running and people are shooting, because now I look like one of them. And someone gets me in the leg. I don't see who. I wasn't lying about that. I'm running down the middle of the highway, people in their cars, shouting at me, shooting, beeping their horns, it's chaos.

My leg is bleeding, but I'm still running. And my buddy, Tom, is with me. We took off together, but I don't remember talking about it. We saw the kids getting shot on the highway, blood spilling out of them, skulls cracking on the pavement. People getting out of their cars and kicking them, hitting them over and over again. Trying to run them over. And everywhere there's this sound – the edge of broken bones being dragged along the pavement. Kids carpooling to school, stopping to watch on the edge of the highway in their mom's station wagon. Fogging up the window. These kids don't remember what a highway looks like without blood on the road.

Tom and I are running and we've stopped looking behind us, 'cause there's nothing to see. And suddenly, Tom is gone. I don't see him anywhere. This is a guy I knew from grade school – joined with me so I wouldn't have to be alone. And he's just gone.

There are bodies on the road, bodies in blown-up buildings. I'm out in the open in the middle of an air strike. Our guys, their guys, I don't know who's bombing but I'm gonna get myself killed. So I get up, and I go into one of the buildings, across the street there – a library, I think. There's a hole the size of a truck in the middle of it. I find a guy, just a guy who was checking out books. He's dead. So I take his clothes. I know I have to blend in. But there's no one to blend in with. Everybody's dead. So I run. I don't have anything left in me. But I run. That's what you would do. I ran.

(There is a long pause. EMMA looks at him.)

EMMA. My mom is gonna wonder where I am.

(EMMA exits.)

(A long moment of LOUIS alone on stage. This could be the last moment of his life. The door opens. LOUIS looks up.)

LOUIS. Marco?

(MARCO steps through the door, holding a large frying pan next to his leg. He is wide-eyed. He looks like a little boy.)

(They stare at each other.)

(Over the loud-speaker, we hear a voice. It starts quietly but gets louder and louder until is it booming all around us.)

VOICE. Hello? Hello. Anybody there? I'd like to get a number three and a medium Coke. Hello? Hello-o. Hello?

MARCO *slowly advances. He raises the frying pan.*

(blackout)

End of Play